This book is dedicated to my Kayla Wayla–the little girl who loves to pack her lunch five minutes before it's time to go. You will always be the peanut butter to my jelly.

Special Thanks

To my girls, Talavia and Brielle–thank you for being my motivation and inspiring me to finish what I started.

Thank you to my family and friends for your support throughout this journey.

Thank you to my book consultant, T. A. Acker, for working so diligently on this project.

To all my readers–thank you for your support. This is only the beginning. Stay tuned!

Minor, M.

Peanut Butter and Jelly for Lunch:

ISBN: 9781095706954

PEANUT BUTTER

BUTTER and

JELLY for LUNCH

I like peanut butter and jelly sandwiches for lunch.
Some days I like it a little bit, some days I like it a lot.

Some days it is my favorite.
Some days it is not.

Some days
I like it with
bananas and
marshmallows
on top.

Some days I like it with the crust on and some days I do not.

On Mondays, I like it with extra jelly. I add more and more until the sides are oozing out.

Mama always shouts,
"Be careful, don't get it on the floor."

"Yes, ma'am," I reply, and add some more.

On Tuesdays, I like my peanut butter and jelly sandwich toasted.

The same way I like my tacos.

I taste a small piece to make sure it's right.

Then I add tomatoes on top.

It gives it a tangy taste.

I have milk for my drink.

Here comes wacky Wednesdays.

I add sprinkles.

Wednesday's are my favorite.

I make cute designs, only to eat them all up.

Sprinkles always go better on top of the jelly and under the peanut butter.

Thursdays seem to roll around fast. I have my peanut butter and jelly in a hurry. On Thursdays, I like to have strawberry jelly instead of grape. I cut my sandwich into perfect shapes.

Some days I like peanut butter and jelly sandwiches a little bit. Some days I like it a lot.

Some days peanut butter and jelly sandwiches are my favorite.

But, on Fridays I'd rather not!

The End

About the Author

Makeia H. Minor is a new, up-and-coming children's author. She was born and raised in the heart of Savannah, Georgia, where she currently resides. Ms. Minor has a passion for children and their education. She has a Bachelor's degree in Criminal Justice and currently pursuing a Master's degree in Education. *Peanut Butter and Jelly for Lunch* is the first of many children's stories to come.

Made in the USA
Columbia, SC
02 August 2020